This book belongs to

ISBN 0 361 06273 7

Published 1984 by Purnell Books, Paulton,
Bristol BS18 5LQ, a member of the BPCC group.
Phototypeset by Quadraset Limited
Made and printed in Great Britain

Tales from Dreamland

Stories by Jane Carruth

Illustrations by Diane Matthes

Purnell

Jessica Mary's Dream

Once upon a time a little girl called Jessica Mary had a very strange dream. First a parrot, with brightly coloured wings, came tapping at her window. "Come with me, Jessica Mary," he said. And Jessica Mary climbed on his back and was whisked away to Fairyland. Once there, she met the King and Queen of Fairyland and one or two of the parrot's special friends. Then the parrot gave

Well, the strange thing is Jessica Mary has a bright blue parrot's feather in her bead box and a ring with a blue stone in it — though her Mummy says the feather was found among the flowers and the ring came out of a Christmas cracker. What do you think?

her one of his bright blue feathers to put in her golden hair. And the young Fairy Prince gave her a very pretty ring with a blue stone in it to wear on her finger.

When it was time to go home, her friend, the parrot, flew back with her and left her safely in bed.

The Fairy Queen's Tea-party

One day the Fairy Queen invited the Tulip Fairies and the Rose Fairies and the Daffodil Fairies to tea in the royal gardens. The Fairies were very excited. But some of the other Flower Fairies were vey upset. "She didn't ask ME!" said the Pansy Fairy; "And she didn't ask ME," said the scarlet Poppy Fairy. "Let's sit on the palace wall and watch the tea-party!"

So that is just what they did. "Go away," cried the Tulip Fairies. "You are not wanted here!"

"We are the Queen's

favourites!" said the Rose Fairies.

But the Queen herself said, "No, let them stay. They must really want to come to tea if they can put up with sitting on that hard stone wall."

"We do want to come to tea," said Pansy and Poppy together.

And they flew down and sat beside the Queen, which made the other Flower Fairies quite annoyed.

Still, it was a lovely tea-party, and Poppy and Pansy are still talking about it!

The Tired Little Elf

Once upon a time there was a little elf. One day he went for a walk in the woods to look for bluebells for his Mummy. He took a big basket with him. But the little elf couldn't find any bluebells to put in his basket.

And at last he sat down. He was so tired that he couldn't walk any more.

"What is the matter?" a big old snail asked.

"I can't find any bluebells for my Mummy," said the little elf, looking very sad. "And now I'm too tired to walk all the way home."

"Climb on my back," said the kindly snail. "I'll take you home."

So the little elf climbed

on the snail's back. The snail knew a quick way home through the woods and, what do you think, there was a patch of pretty bluebells growing by the side of the path!

The little elf quickly filled his basket. Now he was happy again. And so was his Mummy when she saw him. "Make yourself at home

among the lettuces," she said to the kind snail. "Eat all you want."

No wonder the snail was happy too.

The Little White Rabbit in Fairyland

One day Philip's little white rabbit ran away. In the woods he dug a very big hole and made a long, deep tunnel and, do you know, the tunnel was so long and deep it took that little white rabbit straight into Fairyland.

The elves chased the little white rabbit round and round

the toadstools and the fairies threw petals at him as he hopped past. And soon that little white rabbit wished he had stayed in his cosy hutch where it was nice and safe.

Well, the little rabbit was lucky, for he found the entrance to his long, deep tunnel before the elves did and he made his escape. How glad he was to scamper home! But, oh dear, when Philip came to feed him his lettuce leaves — it was Philip's turn to get a shock. His beautiful little white rabbit was no longer white. He was covered with splashes and dashes of yellow and scarlet and blue; the fairy petals had stained his lovely coat with their colours. Philip couldn't understand it! Of course, the little white rabbit could have explained but he decided to keep very silent and let Philip work it out for himself!

The Dance of the Fairies

One very hot sunny afternoon a little boy called Michael was sitting in the garden in his own special chair, watching the butterflies. There was so many of them, mostly white, fluttering and hovering above the flowers.

Then something strange and wonderful happened. All the white butterflies changed into fairies. And they were soon joined by some brown and orange elves who, not long ago, had been handsome brown and orange butterflies.

"We could dance if we had some music," said one of the elves.

"Wait a minute!" Michael shouted. "I'll fetch my recorder!" As soon as Michael started playing, the fairies and elves joined hands and began such a merry dance. But when Michael's Mummy came to see why Michael was playing his recorder, they all changed into butterflies again and flew away. He was just going to explain about the dance of the fairies — then wisely changed his mind!

Elgin had Nowhere to Go

There was once a little elf called Elgin who wouldn't build a house for himself like all the other elves. Instead, he spent most of his time sitting under a large mushroom.

"You'll be sorry one day," said his friends.

"No, I won't," said Elgin. "I'm having fun doing NOTHING."

Well, one day it rained and rained and rained. This doesn't often happen in Fairyland but it does sometimes. All the other little elves rushed into their houses and shut their doors tight. Poor little Elgin had nowhere to go and his big fat mushroom slowly, slowly fell to pieces.

"Oh dear, oh dear!" Elgin cried. "I'm wet through and I have nowhere to go. I wish I had built myself a proper house."

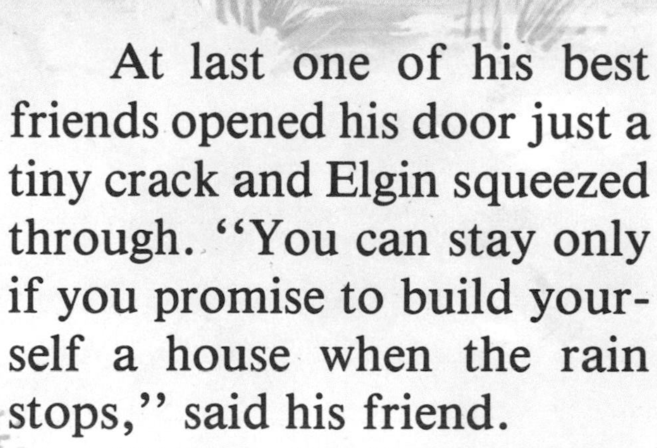

At last one of his best friends opened his door just a tiny crack and Elgin squeezed through. "You can stay only if you promise to build yourself a house when the rain stops," said his friend.

"I promise," said Elgin. And he kept his promise. So whenever it rains Elgin has SOME-WHERE to go.

The Fairy on the Christmas Tree

Have you ever seen a fairy on a Christmas Tree? Most likely you have. Anyway, this is a story about a fairy on a Christmas Tree, which stood in a toyshop window. And it didn't get sold for Christmas.

The fairy was cross. "My beautiful silver wings and tinsel will not last," she grumbled to the tree. "I simply can't stay with you until next Christmas. And just think, I haven't had a single party!"

The tree was sad when he heard this. He really loved the dainty little fairy. Then something quite wonderful happened. Two, maybe three, weeks after Christmas a lady came into the toyshop.

"Have you got such a thing as a Christmas Tree with a fairy on top?" she asked the toyman.

"That's funny," said the toyman. "This very day I was just going to send my last Christmas Tree back to the factory. But I still have it. I put it away in the backshop."

"I'm giving a very late Christmassy kind of party for the orphanage children," said the lady. "They all had measles and mumps over Christmas."

So after all, the fairy on the Christmas Tree had a proper Christmas Party and so, of course, did the tree!

Michael's Granny and the Fairy Cakes

Michael had a Granny who knew so many stories about elves and fairies that Michael thought she must have been to Fairyland. One day when he went to visit her — there she was in the kitchen making cakes.

"These are going to be Fairy Cakes," she said, with twinkling eyes. "When they are ready, you can have one and make a wish, if you like. Maybe and maybe not the

fairies will hear you making it.''

Michael waited patiently until the cakes were ready; then they had to be cooled on a tray before Granny allowed him to have one.

''I'm making my wish,'' said Michael, as he took his first bite. ''I'm wishing and wishing that my Gran will love me for ever and ever.''

Wasn't that a lovely wish? No wonder Michael's Granny smiled happily.

''That's just the kind of wish the fairies like to hear,'' she said at last, and she gave Michael a big hug.

Sophie and the Fairy

Once upon a time a little girl called Sophie went down to the bottom of her garden and met a fairy. The fairy was on a cabbage leaf and Sophie knew she was a fairy because of her silver wings.

"Hi!" said Sophie. "Are you lost or looking for something?"

"I'm looking for something," said the fairy. "I'm looking for one of our caterpillars. He ran away."

"Cabbage leaves are a good place to look for caterpillars," said Sophie. "Has he got red spots or maybe pink ones?" And she giggled.

"He has red and green stripes," said the fairy seriously. "He pulls the Queen's coach when she goes abroad on state occasions."

"Goodness!" Sophie exclaimed. "We must find him."

Sophie began to look under all the cabbage leaves. She saw lots of caterpillars but not one was striped. Then suddenly — there he was, hiding away under an enormous cabbage leaf.

The fairy was delighted. She fixed a silver cord round the naughty caterpillar and told him he was going back to Fairyland. "It's not far," she said, turning to Sophie. "I'll take you there myself one day."

"I'd love that," said Sophie. "Make it soon!" Then she rushed up the garden to tell Mummy about the fairy.

George and the Fairy Pancakes

There was once a little boy called George who loved to eat pancakes. One day he ate a great many pancakes and then went outside and fell asleep under the cherry tree.

Quite soon George began to dream that he was in a big kitchen with lots of fairies and elves rushing about. They were all wearing high chefs' hats and long white aprons. The elves were shouting at the fairies and the fairies were shouting back.

"Whatever is the matter?" George asked.

"The King has ordered one hundred pancakes for his daughter's wedding," said the biggest of the elves. "We really don't know where to start. We don't even know how to make pancakes."

"Making pancakes is easy," laughed George. "I'll show you!" and he got some flour and milk and showed the head cook how to make pancakes.

"You must stay on," said the elfin cook, when he had a hundred fairy pancakes piled high on pretty flowered plates. "Help yourself!"

"I'll make my own," said George. And he did, and he was just in the middle of eating his forty-second fairy pancake when he woke up.

Rachel's Lavender Fairy

Once upon a time the Lavender Fairy whispered in Rachel's ear whilst she was asleep. "Will you please put some of your Mummy's lavender in little bags for me . . .?"

In the morning when Rachel was in the garden, she remembered what the Fairy had said and she asked her Mummy if she could put some of the lavender in little bags for the fairies.

"Yes," said Mummy. And she gave Rachel some pieces of pretty cotton which she didn't want. "Make the bags out of the cotton," she said, "and tie them with some of your old ribbons."

So Rachel spent the morning making bags of lavender for the Fairy. Then she put them in a neat row on the grass. And, do you know, that afternoon when Rachel and her Mummy were out shopping, the Lavender Fairy came with her little barrow and took them all away. In their place, she left a little lavender letter which said, "Thank you very much. Your friend, the Lavender Fairy."

You can just imagine how pleased Rachel was!

Sleepyhead's Dream Boat

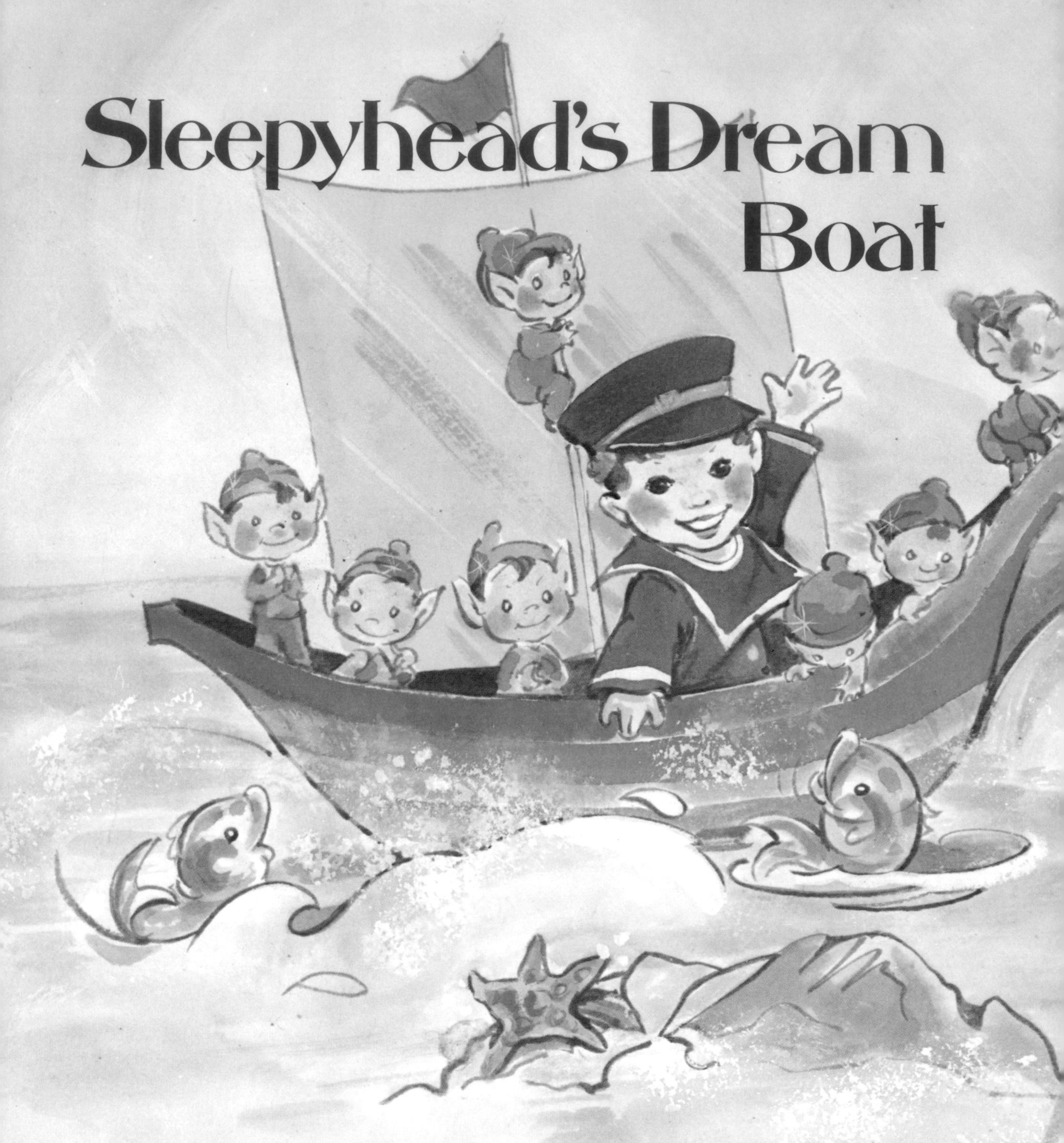

This is the very last story in the book. It is about a little boy whose Mummy called him 'Sleepyhead' because he didn't like getting out of bed in the morning.

Then one night Sleepyhead had a wonderful dream. He went sailing away down the river in a blue and pink boat with a yellow sail. Two little elves in green were the crew and Sleepyhead was the captain. What a super time he

had! He wanted it to go on for ever and ever. And just when the beautiful boat was heading for the open sea, there was a voice crying, "Wake up, Sleepyhead!"

Sleepyhead didn't want to wake up. But when his Mummy whispered that his sailor uncle was home and waiting to take him for a trip on the river, Sleepyhead was out of bed in a flash.

"I was a captain not long ago," Sleepyhead told his uncle, as he climbed aboard the pleasure steamer.

"I hope you had some good sailors," said his uncle.

"Oh, I did," said Sleepyhead. "They were elves, you see!"